The List

by Hazel Hutchins
art by Maria van Lieshout

annick press
toronto + new york + vancouver

Annick Press Ltd.

We acknowledge the support of the Canada Council for the Arts, the Ontario Arts Council, and the Government of Canada through the Book Publishing Industry Development Program (BPIDP) for our publishing activities.

Cataloging in Publication

Hutchins, H. J. (Hazel J.)
     The list / by Hazel Hutchins ; art by Maria van Lieshout.

ISBN-13: 978-1-55451-064-1 (bound)
ISBN-10: 1-55451-064-3 (bound)
ISBN-13: 978-1-55451-063-4 (pbk.)
ISBN-10: 1-55451-063-5 (pbk.)

    I. Van Lieshout, Maria   II. Title.

PS8565.U826L57 2007   jC813'.54   C2006-903765-5

Distributed in Canada by:
Firefly Books Ltd.
66 Leek Crescent
Richmond Hill, ON
L4B 1H1

Published in the U.S.A. by:
Annick Press (U.S.) Ltd.
Distributed in the U.S.A. by:
Firefly Books (U.S.) Inc.
P.O. Box 1338
Ellicott Station
Buffalo, NY 14205

Printed in China.

Visit us at: www.annickpress.com

For Kassidy, Corteney, Jaiden and
Nessa. And with thanks to Tara and JP.
—H.H.

To Ammie and in memory of Appie.
With cartfuls of love.
—M.V.L.

There was once a tiny kingdom that was known for its kindness — always first to help its neighbors in times of need, always first to congratulate them in times of joy. One day it sent joyful news of its own: *A royal baby has been born in the kingdom of Thibodeau!*

Far away, in the land of Iddison, the Queen was delighted.

"We shall make a trip to help them celebrate," she announced. "We shall bring the child splendid gifts from our own land, and along the way we shall gather all the marvels of our travels as well."

The Queen began to make a list, for she did not want
to miss any of the marvels. The royal daughter, Cassidy,
began to make a list too. This made her mother smile,
because Cassidy was a very little princess and had only
learned to print things like the letters of the alphabet and
her name, which often came out in a rather backward,
upside-down fashion like this:

$$\text{CASSIDY (mirror-reversed)}$$

Cassidy paid no attention to her mother's smile. She
carefully finished her list and put it in her pocket.

On the day of departure, everyone gathered in the courtyard.

There were prancing horses for the travelers and sturdy ox carts for their supplies. There were eight great elephants pulling eight enormous wagons, two for the treasures from their own kingdom and six for the treasures they would find along the way.

The Queen looked at her list
and nodded.
Cassidy looked at her list
and nodded too, though she
rode on her pony with only
her teddy bear and one small
bundle containing a change of
clothes and a toothbrush.

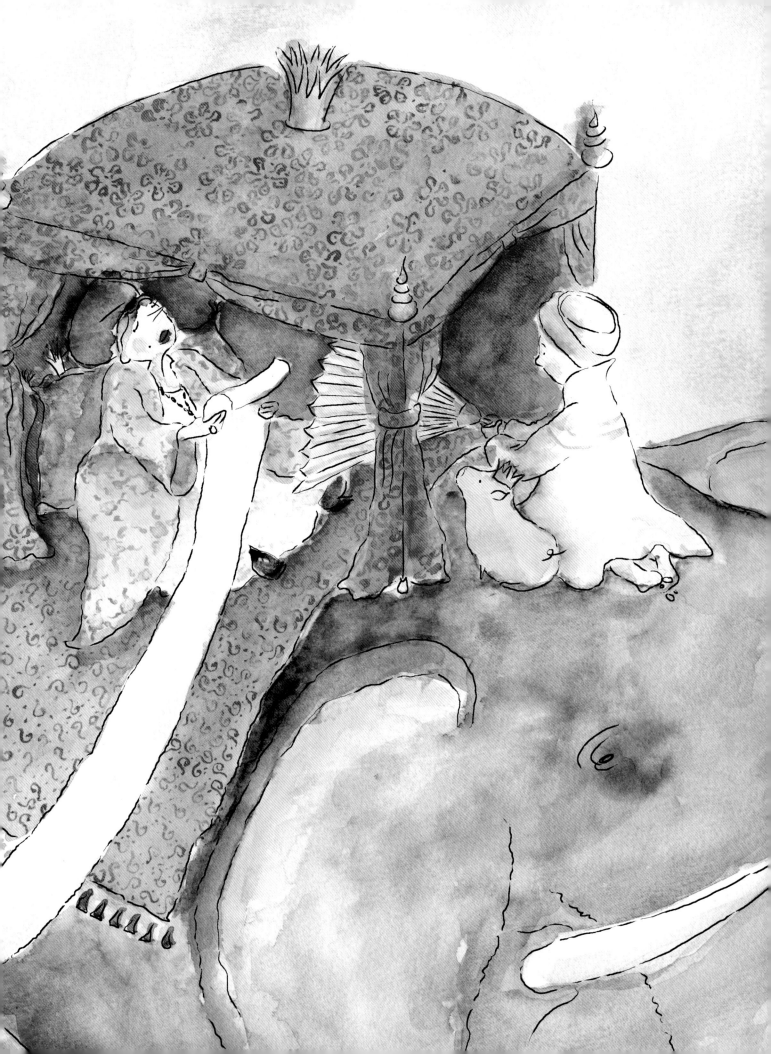

Across their own kingdom they traveled. They
gathered the finest vegetables, seeds, and livestock.
Toy makers added intricate inventions. Teachers and
entertainers brought beautiful books and instruments.

The Queen paid handsomely and the people them-
selves added many more items, for there was not a
person in all the lands who had not felt the kindness
of the kingdom of Thibodeau at one time or another.

Up the great mountains they climbed. In the high mines the wagons were laden with precious stones and splendid jewelry. In the valleys the warmest wools, the softest cottons, and the shiniest silks were added.

The Queen looked at her list and nodded. Cassidy looked at her list and nodded too, though she still rode with only her teddy bear and one small bundle containing a change of clothes and a toothbrush.

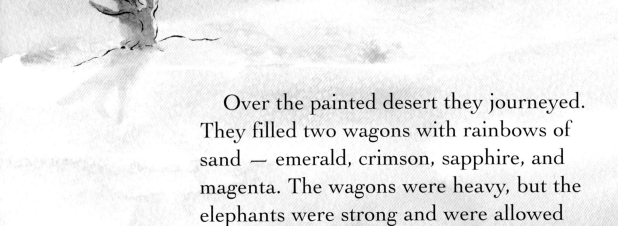

Over the painted desert they journeyed.
They filled two wagons with rainbows of
sand — emerald, crimson, sapphire, and
magenta. The wagons were heavy, but the
elephants were strong and were allowed
to travel at their own pace.

Lastly, in a dense jungle, they gathered exotic wood and astounding flowers. Parrots and monkeys joined the caravan, and even great jaguars climbed aboard, although they had to promise not to eat the monkeys or the courtiers or the royal baby.

The Queen thanked everyone. She looked at her list and nodded. Cassidy looked at her list and nodded too, though she still rode with only her teddy bear and one small bundle containing a change of clothes and a toothbrush.

After many days they arrived, at dusk, in the kingdom of Thibodeau. The castle was alive with light and color. The great procession was brought into the courtyard and the gifts were presented.

First were the gifts from Iddison itself.
"How can we ever thank you," said the
Queen of Thibodeau. "The royal child will
always be wonderfully fed and will always
have food for the mind as well."

Next were the jewels and fabrics of the mountains. "How warmly and beautifully dressed our child will be," said the King. "All children in Thibodeau shall share in the generosity of these gifts."

Now came the sands of the desert.
"What truly royal colors for the baby's artistic explorations!" exclaimed the royal art tutor.

Then came the treasures of the jungle.
"The most beautiful of surroundings and the most
amusing of playmates," declared the royal nursemaid.
"What more could any baby want?"

Which is when Cassidy reached into her pocket and took out her list.

And when her mother saw what the royal daughter had written, she felt both foolish and proud. What other gifts could be more wonderful? What other letters could be as perfect, even when written backwards and upside down?

Cassidy stepped forward and very gently
gave the royal baby

two kisses ✕ ✕
and one hug ○

And everyone who was there will tell you
that, in spite of all the fancy gifts the baby
received, it was not until this moment that
the best part happened ...

The royal baby smiled its very first smile.